Erin Dealey

The HALF BIRTHDAY BOOK

Illustrated by
Germán Blanco

For PZapp, G & Scotty
With special thanks to Deborah Warren
and Karen Kilpatrick
and a shout out to Mr. Douty
:)

 Genius Cat Books

www.geniuscatbooks.com
Parkland, FL

ABOUT THIS BOOK

The art for this book was created with photoshop and illustrator, using a Wacom Cintiq. Text was set in Providence Sans Pro, New Kansas and Avenir Next. It was designed by Germán Blanco.
Text copyright © 2023 by Erin Dealey.
Illustrations copyright © 2023 by Germán Blanco.

Library of Congress Control Number: 2022935090
ISBN: 978-1-938447-55-6 (hardcover)
First edition, 2023
Our books may be purchased in bulk for promotional, educational, or business use. For more information, or to schedule an event, please visit geniuscatbooks.com.
Printed and bound in China.

Erin Dealey

The HALF BIRTHDAY BOOK

Illustrated by
Germán Blanco

Not many have seen the HALF Birthday Buddies.

In fact, they're quite sneaky that way.

But early one morning you might wake to find

It's your Happiest $\frac{1}{2}$ Birthday!

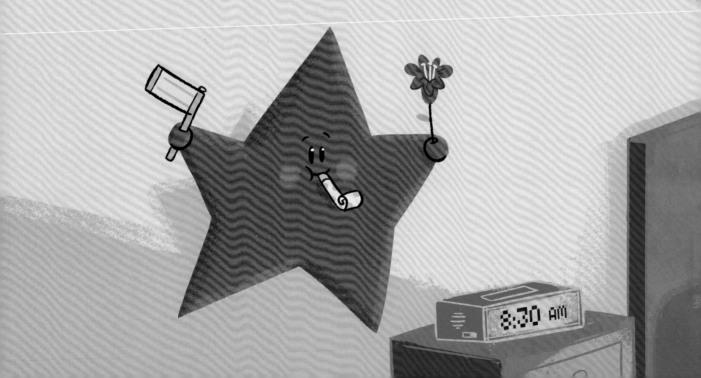

Are there HALF streamers decorating HALF of the room?

Small balloons only HALF-filled with air?

You might think you're dreaming, or still HALF asleep.

Nope! The HALF Birthday Buddies were there.

How do they do that?

Who are these Buddies that stir up
such HALF Birthday fun?

Ready buddies?

Shhhhh...

They meet in the moonlight, at HALF Birthday homes,

At precisely HALF past one...

Best Buddy tiptoes around in the dark
to make sure no one's HALF awake!

Blinger whispers a lullaby
filled with sweet dreams.

I GOT CATITUDE!

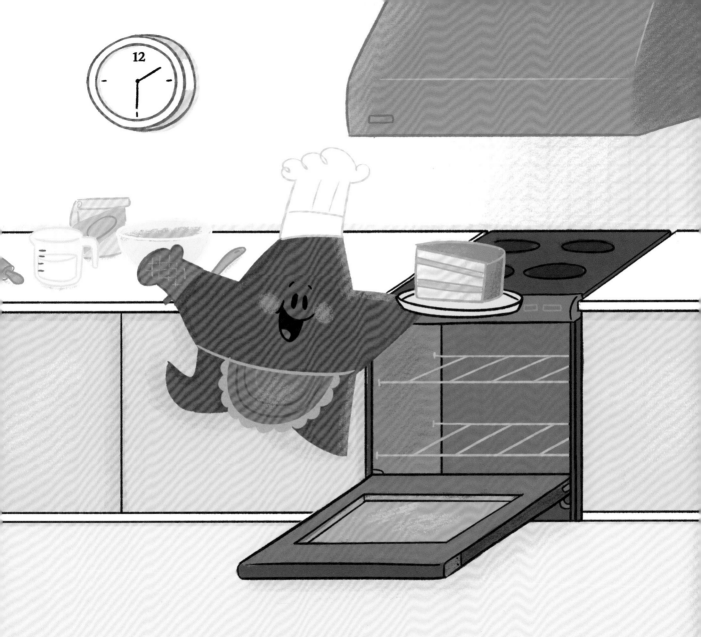

While Big Buddy bakes a
HALF cake!

Bright makes these HALF invitations:

Let's **PARTY!**

What to wear:

Dress HALF right &

HALF wrong.

The Buddies will hide when you open your eyes.

But you might hear their HALF birthday song...

Hap___ HALF ___Day ___ you!

Hap___ HALF ___Day ___ you!

Hap___ HALF ___Day ___you!

Time for
HALF Birthday fun
with your family and friends
on this special day just for **YOU.**

The **HALF** Birthday Buddies have left you a list.

Which crazy things will **you** do?

Watch HALF a movie and guess how it ends.

Hı –5!

Play HALF of a game—winner-winner!

Finish these sentences, HALF Birthday friends:

I love Half Birthdays because _____.

My Half Birthday is on _____.

(Hint: add 6 months to your actual birthday!)

Eat half of a sandwich for dinner!

Want to make hats for your HALF Birthday Bash?

(Every HALF Birthday Buddy has one!)

Roll up some paper in the shape of a cone,

Then decorate HALF and you're done!

No presents allowed. Not even HALF ones.

Just this WHOLE book of HALF things to do!

Hip Hip, _____!!!

HALF-cheers for a Happy HALF Birthday

From the HALF Birthday Buddies to YOU.

Hip Hip,

_____!!!

Hip

Hip,

_____!!!

Did you notice any half objects?

HALF PAINT

HALF PAST THE HOUR

HALF VASE

HALF GLASS

HALF LAMP

HALF JUICE

HALF DOG

HALF GIFT

HALF NOTE

HALF MOON

Can you find the other halves?

When to celebrate your HALF Birthday:

My real birthday:

_____ (Month / Day)

+ Add six months!

= My HALF Birthday:

_____

This whole
1/2 BIRTHDAY BOOK
is for

_____.

Dear reader,

We hope you enjoyed this book!

If you purchased this book from a place where you can leave a review, we would greatly appreciate it if you would give us your honest feedback. It helps the book reach more readers and we love hearing from you!

Please join us on Instagram or Facebook:

@geniuscatbooks

We'll do our best to make it fun!

With love,

 Genius Cat Books